Written by **Warren Nelson**

Illustrated by **Karlyn Holman**

Bayfield Street Publishing

Washburn, Wisconsin

Bayfield Street Publishing, Inc.
405 West 5th Street
Washburn, WI 54891
(715)-373-1040

Ditch of Witches
FIRST EDITION

10 9 8 7 6 5 4 3 2 1

Editorial Director: John Teeter
Typography & layout:
Ros Nelson, Watermark MN Inc.

Library of Congress
Catalog Card Number 99-61576
ISBN 0-9670683-0-4
Printed in Canada
by Friesens; Altona, Manitoba

Acknowledgements

Many gifted and generous people have helped me with this adventure. First of all, I would like to thank the "witches," Mary Rice, Patsy Avery, Betty Ferris and my sister Jacki King. Also Warren Nelson, Jack Gunderson, John and Renee Teeter, Kris Engfer, Amy Kalmon, Darrelyn Olson, Irene Blakely, Judy Peyton, John Hanson, and my husband Gary Holman.
–Karlyn Holman

My mother, Clestle Loraine Gillespie Nelson, gave the poet tongue to me. She is a natural born storyteller and still the wiggiest chick I ever met. My late father, Alvin Udell Nelson, was the kindest man I ever knew and he let me run through my southern Minnesota boyhood free and easy. This poem was written for the musical, *A Martin County Hornpipe*, first performed in Fairmont, Minnesota in 1976. Thanks to Betty Ferris, partner and mother of my children, for her faith in my writing. Here's to Karlyn Holman and her brush with this world.
–Warren Nelson

Dedications

This book is dedicated to my friend
and fellow artist, Mary Rice,
"the angel of Bayfield."
Mary's kind heart and generous spirit
have enriched all our lives.
– *Karlyn Holman*

To my children, Medora and
Rowan Nelson-Ferris

– *Warren Nelson*

What do witches do after Halloween?

Well, they don't just sit around!

They are hanging out in the ditches

at the edge of your town, stirring up trouble all year.

It is the winter witches who call the blizzard down...

just when you think winter is over.

Stirring the north wind with their switches,

ssssssssss
ssssssssss
sssssssssss
ssssssssssssssss
ssssssssssssssss Stirring snow and cold together

...One bright morning to change the weather!

The oldest coldest witch in the ditch,
The eldest of the sisters said,
"It's half the winter past their Christmas.

Now we call the high winds down,

Down around...and bury the town!"

And in the town
the people unbuttoned.
And busy with busyness,
busy as nickels,

"Good morning" they say when they meet on the street.

"A good morning it is and warm for the season.

No reason for wearing a scarf

or a sweater.

By the look of the sun

it may only get better."

"Ha!" said the oldest witch in the ditch.

"I hate the sun!" said one of her sisters.

"I skate on the moon. The sun gives me blisters!

Here it is March, and we haven't yet

stirred them a blizzard they won't soon forget!"

"Let them hide in their houses!"

She said with a scowl.

Let the wind sting!

and growl and howl

Quick from the north! No mercy or warning!

Shiver and shake the cold bones of the morning!

Down around and cover the ground,

Drifts of snow to bury the town!"

And who heard it first as the witches flew away?

The roads are all closed — No school today!

A Few Words
About Witches

The poem, *Ditch of Witches*, was conceived by Warren Nelson while
stranded aboard a ditch-bound bus during a Minnesota blizzard.
Ditch of Witches was first introduced to the public
as part of Warren Nelson's musical production,
A Martin County Hornpipe, which portrays the history
and folklore of Martin County, Minnesota.

Tales about witches have long been a prominent feature
of the American storytelling landscape. The colorful balls
seen in several illustrations from this story are drawn from
early-American witch lore. Known as witch balls or whimsies,
these spheres of blown glass were hung near doorways by colonist
seeking to protect themselves from the magical wiles of witches.

The people and locations depicted in this book are real.
The four people who served as models for the witches have each made
important contributions to their communities and are not, of course,
actual witches. The locations depicted in this book can be found
on the South Shore of Lake Superior in the towns of Washburn
and Bayfield, Wisconsin.

Lake Superior Big Top Chautauqua

A percentage of the proceeds from this book will be donated
to support the *Lake Superior Big Top Chautauqua*.

Lake Superior Big Top Chautauqua operates an intimate, 750-seat
capacity, professional tent theater, producing and presenting over
seventy summer nights of concerts, plays, lectures, and original
illuminated, historical musicals. Incorporated as a non-profit
organization in 1986, Lake Superior Big Top Chautauqua was founded
in the spirit of turn-of-the-century traveling tent chautauquas that
brought culture to the people of rural America.

The Big Top Chautauqua overlooks Lake Superior in Wisconsin's
northwoods, south of Bayfield, Wisconsin and operates Memorial Day
through Labor Day. For information on our summer schedule, tours,
Tent Show Radio, and to join our mailing list,
call 1-888-244-8368, or visit us on the web at www.bigtop.org .